BOOK ONE

STEPHANIE BAUDET

Published by Sweet Cherry Publishing Limited
Unit E, Vulcan Business Complex
Vulcan Road
Leicester, LE5 3EB
United Kingdom

www.sweetcherrypublishing.com

First published in the UK in 2016
ISBN: 978-1-78226-265-7

© Stephanie Baudet 2016

Illustrations © Allied Artists
Illustrated by Illary Casasanta
Cover design by Andrew Davis

The Dinosaur Detectives: The Amazon Rainforest

Printed and bound by Thomson Press (India) Ltd.

Chapter One

Matt lifted the egg carefully off the table and felt its weight in his hands. It was about fifteen centimetres in diameter, and round, like a small football. Although it was now fossilised, this little egg - if you could call it little - would have hatched into a baby dinosaur and eventually grown into something bigger than anybody today could ever imagine.

But something had happened and this little egg had never hatched. Of course, eggs were food for other dinosaurs, too, but this particular one hadn't been eaten, either.

Matt closed his eyes while his dad looked on with anticipation.

He was now used to the spinning sensation. It had made him feel sick at first but now he knew what to expect. The weight of the fossilised egg

gradually lightened until he was no longer aware that he was holding it. In front of him a forest scene unfolded until it filled his entire field of vision. A bubble of excitement began in his chest and almost exploded as he gazed at the scene. This was far better than a computerised virtual world.

The shape of an enormous sauropod dinosaur grew from a dim shadow in front of him, becoming a sharp, three-dimensional, moving animal, stretching its long leathery neck to reach some leaves at the top of a tree.

It was a titanosaur; a herbivore weighing about fifteen tonnes and approximately seventeen metres long. A gentle giant, some might say, although you wouldn't want to get in the way of those elephant-like feet!

Wow! Matt looked up at it in awe as it chewed its way placidly through a bunch of leaves at the top of a tree. It was so big that he doubted it had any predators.

It seemed unaware of his presence, as they always were, because he wasn't really there at all. Since he'd been about six, when his palaeontologist father had first begun specialising in hunting dinosaur eggs rather than bones, Matt had had this ability to be able to hold an egg and

visualise the dinosaur that would have hatched from it.

He clearly remembered the first time it had happened. He'd been scared to death! At first the visions had been vague and shadowy and only lasted a few seconds. No one had really believed him then, and who could blame them. 'Childish imagination,' they said, but over the years the visions had become more realistic. Firstly came the colour and then the sharper shapes, and eventually they appeared three dimensional.

Not only was Matt's dad a palaeontologist but he was also a palaeo-artist. He painted highly detailed pictures of dinosaurs, mostly with Matt's help. Until now, palaeontologists could only guess what dinosaurs looked like from their skeletons, or sometimes from the embryos still hidden inside the unhatched eggs. But their ideas were often incomplete, or inaccurate.

The titanosaur looked around and then lowered its head to nibble at a small bush. Matt noticed that the leaves looked dry and discoloured instead of lush green. Looking round, it occurred to him that all the vegetation was thin and brownish, as if affected by a disease.

Suddenly, the Titanosaurus was alert and stopped eating, raising its head to look beyond Matt. Matt wondered what had aroused its attention. He didn't have the ability to turn to look. His presence in the prehistoric world was limited to a single view, like watching a film. Maybe one day that would change, too.

It must be something large, because the titanosaur, despite its size, was clearly afraid of it. Matt could see the apprehension in its eyes and the way it raised its head up high to make itself look bigger.

Suddenly, Matt was back in the room with his dad. His time spent in that world was limited and not under his control.

'It was a titanosaur, and something was after it.' He was breathing quickly.

'Maybe a T-Rex,' said Dad, putting a hand on his shoulder. 'The titanosaur was bigger, but if there was more than one T-Rex, he would be in trouble. They couldn't move very fast because he had to keep three feet on the ground at all times. Hefty creatures, but not built for speedy getaways.'

He was silent for a minute. 'But what was its

hide like? And its head? No skulls have been found.'

'The hide was grey and scaly,' said Matt. 'It looked really tough. The skull was small for its size, and quite flat, with a small mouth and single row of small teeth. It had a really long tail and a neck about the same length. Like this.'

Matt began to sketch the animal. He was good at drawing, like his dad.

'If it was a T-Rex coming for the titanosaur,' he said, pausing in his drawing, 'that would put it in the late Cretaceous period, wouldn't it? About 65 million years ago, just before the giant meteor hit the earth and killed them all.'

His dad nodded and smiled. Matt bent to finish his sketch. He couldn't wait to go on a fossil hunt and look for eggs himself.

'But the leaves were all brown,' said Matt. 'And the sky red.'

'Volcanic gases and ash in the atmosphere,' said his dad. 'That happened when what is now India crashed into Asia. The eruptions lasted about 30 thousand years.'

'Wow!' Matt couldn't imagine such a length of time, but that was nothing compared to the millions of years that the dinosaurs ruled the earth. You couldn't get your head round it.

'The earth was dying,' he said. 'Then it was volcanoes and now it's us polluting the air and destroying habitats.' He was silent as he bent to finish the sketch.

CHAPTER TWO

'Whew, it's hot!'

Matt looked scathingly at the girl beside him. 'What do you expect? It's Brazil. We're at the equator.'

'I know, but ...' she tugged at her blue jumper.

Matt gritted his teeth. He had been angry ever since his dad had told him that Jo, his cousin, was coming on the expedition. He was sure that she would ruin it. She'd be complaining about everything as well as asking silly questions. What had Dad been thinking? This was a serious fossil-finding expedition, funded by the Palaeontology Institute and the Brazilian government. Why had Dad brought her along? She didn't know anything about dinosaurs!

'Feeling the heat, Jo?'

Matt rolled his eyes. Now Dad was joining in

on this boring conversation. What was the matter with them?

Here they were at the beginning of a great adventure, and all they could talk about was the weather. That's what you did in Britain, not here. How about, 'Wow! We're in Brazil!'

But Dad was still chatting about the heat. 'Now you know why I suggested you wore layers, even though it's summer in England. It's humid here, that's the trouble.'

They had walked out of the airport into the blazing sunshine. Matt was hot, too, but he resisted the urge to take off his hoodie. He'd only

have to carry it. Anyway, the hotel would be air-conditioned, hopefully.

'There's our driver,' said Dad, pointing to a man standing beside an old black car. He waved and the man came towards them, beaming.

'Senhor Sharp?' he asked.

He took their bags and heaved them into the boot.

The cab was air-conditioned, despite how old it looked, and Matt sank into the soft, worn leather. He was tired after the long flight, and that only made him more irritated.

This should have been the most exciting time of his life – the adventure he'd been waiting for! At last he had reached twelve and could join Dad on his dinosaur fossil expedition. Then, what happened? Jo, his cousin from Canada, was suddenly invited to come along. Her parents were both doctors and were attending a conference in Geneva. She had hurriedly had her vaccinations, bought appropriate clothing, and here she was. And she was only eleven. It wasn't fair! 'When you're twelve,' Dad had always said. 'When you're twelve you can come with me, as long as it's during the school holidays.'

He could feel Jo's gaze on him but he pretended to be looking out of the window. It was a big city, but flat and dusty. There were buildings that looked shabby, but also taller and more modern ones. A low range of grey and green hills stretched across the horizon. That would be the way they were heading tomorrow – into the Amazon rainforest.

Matt felt a flutter of excitement begin in his belly, but then he squashed it. She would be a pain. She would probably hold up the expedition and be afraid of everything.

'Matt, I'm sorry. Don't be mad at me.' It was a shock to find that either she was a mind reader, or his anger showed in his face. Jo put a hand on his arm and he froze. 'This could be fun.'

He turned sharply to face her. 'Fun? This is not meant to be fun. It's not a holiday, it's an expedition. It'll be hard trekking through the rainforest. And you probably have no interest at all in my dad's work.'

He spoke quietly enough so that Dad wouldn't hear him getting angry. He didn't want him to think he was being selfish.

'I am interested in dinosaurs!' said Jo.

'Yeah. I'll bet!'

'Of course, I love Uncle Alan's paintings, too.'

'How many of those have you seen?' He hated to admit it, but she was keeping cool, unlike him.

'Okay, I've only really looked at them online, but

my dad has one. Uncle Alan gave it to him last Christmas. It's the one of the pterodactyl flying through the trees. It's just magical. He captures the atmosphere so well, and the expression on its face.'

Matt bit off the retort he was about to make. Maybe she really did love the painting. His dad got praise from people all over the world! Although no-one knew how he was able to paint them in such detail, they just assumed that it was part imagination and part guesswork from fossils and footprints.

Matt's talent had been kept a secret, and that was the way his parents wanted it to stay – for the moment. When he was older, with his education behind him, he could reveal his gift to the world. At that stage, he hoped he could follow his father into the profession.

Matt took a deep breath and turned back to the window. They were sweeping into the forecourt of a hotel. He was looking forward to getting a good sleep; he'd hardly slept at all on the flight, unlike Jo. He'd watched a movie without really taking it in, his temper brewing up nicely until it was almost at bursting point. It wasn't Jo's fault really, though, it was Dad's. Maybe he shouldn't be so angry with her, as long as she wasn't a nuisance.

Matt reached out and dragged his rucksack nearer to him. He always kept it close. It was full of the tools and important equipment he'd collected over the years. He'd spent many happy hours at the beach fossicking for anything interesting, and he'd always find something he could talk to Dad about. Of course, he'd brought a notepad and pencil, too. He was never without those.

The rest of the team was waiting in the hotel lobby. There were two men and one woman.

The woman rushed forward, her hand outstretched. 'Mr Sharp! I'm so honoured to meet you and to have been asked to join this expedition. I'm a great admirer of your work ...' She was almost grovelling at his feet.

Hold on, thought Matt, Dad'll get big-headed. Just for a moment his usual humour broke through his anger.

It was then that the woman spotted him and Jo. She stared at them, frowning.

'Are these kids with you?'

Meanwhile, the two men shook hands with Matt's dad. One was tall and lean with a crop of red hair.

'Frazer Connolly,' he said, with a definite Scottish accent. 'I'm going to be your interpreter.'

The other man beamed. 'I'm Andrew Smart.

Also delighted to be on this trip. I hope you had a good flight?' His gaze swept over them all. He was friendly and open and looked about Dad's age.

'And I'm Jean Williams,' said the woman, a little calmer now. She swept a stray wisp of blonde hair behind her ear. Her smile seemed a little forced. 'I'm surprised you have brought your children, Mr Sharp. If I'd known this was going to be a children's outing, I would …'

'My son, Matt,' said Dad. 'And my niece, Jo.'

That was all he said. No explanations or apologies to appease her. Just an introduction. Matt felt his anger dissipate a little. He could never stay angry with his dad for long.

Jean Williams gave a tight smile and a shrug of the shoulders, as if it was all the same to her, but she was obviously quite perturbed by the whole thing.

'My God, isn't that …?' Dad was looking beyond the group and towards the lifts. Then he shook his head. 'Sorry. I thought I saw someone I used to know.' He hesitated. 'If you'll excuse us, I'll just get these two up to their rooms and then we can talk.'

As they walked away Matt glanced back and saw the look Jean Williams was giving them as she spoke to Frazer and Andrew. He knew she

was complaining about them being there, but his dad was the leader of the expedition, and he, Matt, would show them that he wasn't just a waste of space.

After checking in, they went up to their rooms. Jo had a single room to herself, which might have given Matt another cause to be annoyed with her, but then he remembered that he would have been sharing with Dad whether she had come or not. He smiled smugly at the look on Jo's face as she closed the door to her room.

'Sleep well,' said Dad from the doorway as Matt threw his bag on one of the two beds. 'We've got an early start tomorrow and a long way to go.' He grinned. 'Excited?'

Matt nodded. 'Dad, who was that person you saw in the lobby?'

His father frowned, shaking his head. 'It couldn't have been who I thought it was. Just someone I used to know at university – but that was quite a few years ago. Get some sleep, Son.'

Matt sighed. He would have to make the best of it, he supposed. But if that girl did anything to ruin this expedition, he would never forgive her. His dad had just been awarded an MBE by the Queen, so his reputation was hanging on this trip.

CHAPTER THREE

'Just a wee briefing before we leave,' said Frazer Connolly. They were all squeezed around a table, and Frazer stood at the head with his hands on his hips.

They'd had a good breakfast and were packed and ready to go. It was only seven-thirty in the morning! Matt flattened his scruffy hair with his hand and yawned, still jet-lagged. Frazer looked at him and frowned.

'This is no walk in the park,' Frazer began, his gaze lingering on Matt for a moment before sweeping round to encompass the whole group. 'It's hot, humid weather for one thing, and the rainforest holds many dangers. Which creature do you think is the most dangerous?' He gave the impression of talking to the whole group, but

Matt guessed that he probably meant him and Jo, especially.

'Jaguars,' said Matt. He would show that he'd researched the area before they left.

Frazer shook his head. 'Anyone else?'

'Venomous snakes,' said Matt's dad.

'No.'

'Poisonous spiders?' asked Jo.

'They are all dangerous,' said Frazer. 'But they will try to get out of your way, they won't attack you.' He looked round the group to make sure everyone was listening. 'The deadliest creatures are mosquitoes.'

'But we've had our malaria vaccinations,' Jean said.

'Mosquitoes also carry other diseases, especially dengue fever. That's not usually fatal, but it's serious and there is no vaccine against it or any treatment, which is why we must protect against it. Unlike the other creatures, mosquitoes are always out to get you.' He looked at Jean. 'You'll need to wear a long-sleeved shirt over that vest. Something light-coloured – mosquitoes are attracted to dark colours.'

'But … it'll be hot.' She pouted, like an enraged child.

'Long sleeves,' repeated Frazer, 'and when we

set off into the rainforest, tuck your trousers into your boots.' He looked around at everyone's footwear but said nothing, so it must have met with his approval. A bit late now for going out and buying new gear, thought Matt.

'There are many dangerous creatures in the rainforest,' continued Frazer. 'Some have been mentioned already, so here are the rules:

'Check your boots before you put them on each day. Something might have crawled inside. Wear a big hat at all times – against the sun and also against snakes that might have dropped down from the trees. Don't paddle in the river to cool your feet. There are piranhas, as well as large stingrays. The locals call them wish-you-were-dead fish, so that says it all. Always be careful where you walk. There is a venomous snake called a lancehead, which likes to lie on man-made paths and looks very much like dead leaves.'

Everyone was quiet and Matt stole a look at Jo. She looked pale, but he didn't feel smug about it. He felt pale himself! No amount of research could make him feel better about facing these things for real.

Frazer gave a faint smile. 'That's it for the moment. It's a lot to take in and I'll give you more information as we go along. Just keep your wits about you and don't touch anything.'

'There's more?' whispered Jo. 'How does he know all this?'

'He's spent a lot of time here,' Matt's dad said. 'He speaks Portuguese fluently and a couple of the local languages, too. He's not a professional palaeontologist, but a naturalist who is interested in fossils.'

'I'm sure all that advice won't be needed,' commented Jo, in an off-hand manner. 'He probably enjoys telling people about the dangers just to see them get scared.'

But before the rainforest trek there was a long drive ahead. They were taking two vehicles – four-by-four trucks – and Matt and Jo were directed into one of them. It was inevitable that they would have to sit together.

Dad had been strangely quiet since they'd got up and Matt wondered what was worrying him. Was he regretting bringing him and Jo along? He hoped it was just Jo that he regretted bringing. Matt was always a good companion! At least, he tried to be.

All the same, there was something on Dad's mind. He was never moody and had endless enthusiasm for his work. He was usually on a high just before an expedition, but even now he was looking behind them as they pulled out of the hotel forecourt. Did he think someone was following them?

Matt thought back to the man in the lobby. Was it the man Dad had known at university? And if so, why was it a bad thing to see an old friend? Matt put it out of his mind for the moment; he didn't want to be distracted whilst they were trekking through the rainforest! If it was really a problem, he was sure his dad would tell him.

The road began as tarmac but eventually became little more than a dirt track. They were following the River Itapecuru and had passed through a few small towns with colourful and run-down houses, some with grass roofs, others orange tiles.

Children in dirty ragged clothes played in the street and watched them as they passed. They had been surrounded by the rainforest for all of their lives, Matt thought, and might never have been outside their village.

Matt and Jo didn't talk much. Matt's anger had lessened, but he still resented Jo being there. He hadn't spoken to Dad about it, not even when he first told them Jo was coming. He could usually talk to Dad easily, but somehow couldn't tell

him how he felt about this. He thought that Dad would have known how important this trip was to him. Every birthday he had pleaded with Dad to let him accompany him, and every birthday Dad had smiled and said, 'When you're twelve.'

Late in the day they finally stopped in a small town outside what Frazer called 'our hotel'. It was a single-storey building that had once been white, but was now more of a brown colour. It hardly looked big enough to accommodate their small group, let alone any other guests.

As Matt stepped out of the car he noticed that the dry ground had been churned up as though some large vehicles had been here after the rain. There were big tyre tracks, too, imprinted in the dried mud, but Matt was too tired to give them much thought. He just wanted to get to a comfy bed!

Inside the lobby there was no air conditioning, just a large fan in the centre of the ceiling, creaking as it rotated. It was the same in the bedrooms. There were, Matt noticed when they went up to bed, screens on the windows to keep out the mosquitos (and other insects), so at least they could be left open during the night.

Before they settled down to sleep, Matt had to ask what was worrying his dad.

'Was it that man you saw in the hotel?'

He watched Dad's reaction as he sat down heavily on the bed. His usual bright enthusiasm had gone from his face, and been replaced by a worried frown. He hesitated before speaking, as if wondering how much to tell Matt.

'It seems we're in a race,' he said. 'I tried to hire a helicopter to get us there quicker, but there wasn't one available at such short notice.'

'A helicopter? But that would mean we wouldn't

have trekked through the rainforest.'

'That's right,' said his dad. 'But the reason for this expedition is to hunt for dinosaur eggs. The trek through the forest was a means of getting there without incurring too much expense. Now, I wish we had gone by helicopter in the first place.'

'But who is that man, Dad?'

'Frank Hellman, a fellow student from university, as I said. He wanted all the recognition and acclaim without putting in the work. Oh, he scraped through his degree, but then resented the fact that others, especially me, had papers published in prestigious journals, and funding to do our work. And now, with my MBE ...'

'He wants to find the dinosaur eggs first?' said Matt.

His dad nodded. 'He's funding himself, so he has to get his hands on them – if indeed there are any – so that he can sell them to private collectors for a lot of money. That's what I'm guessing, anyway.' He stood up. 'Come on, into bed. We've a big day tomorrow.'

Matt was silent. He knew it was no good pushing Dad for more information, but he couldn't resist one more question. 'Did he talk to you?'

His dad nodded. 'Briefly. He just said, "This one's mine, Sharp, and ..."'

'And?'

'That was all,' said Dad, but Matt knew that it wasn't. He just didn't want to worry him. Well, Dad might be able to let it go, but Matt was certainly not going to let Frank Hellman beat them. This was turning into more than an expedition.

The next morning the vehicles took them a few miles until the track petered out. Matt jumped out, landing in a squelchy patch of wet mud. He was immediately aware of the dense forest around them. The humidity made it almost difficult to breathe and he could feel sweat breaking out on his body already. There was the constant noise of unfamiliar birds, and he looked up at the dark green canopy of leaves high above.

Matt couldn't help grinning. This time he didn't try to suppress the thrill of excitement. They were here at last, in the Amazon rainforest, setting out for the fossil dig site, and he couldn't believe it! Recently, fossils had been found by students on a rainforest trekking holiday. Given the climate, it was an unusual place for fossils to exist. The animal had been named Amazonsaurus maranhensis. It had lived in the early Cretaceous period between 125 and 100 million years ago, and was a herbivore, around twelve metres long and weighing five tonnes; a gentle giant, like the

titanosaur, whose egg he had held and 'seen' in the vision.

The trekkers had passed on the information to the Palaeontologists' Society and the actual location had been kept secret to all but a few, which included, of course, the Brazilian government who was funding their expedition.

Two local men from the town where they had stayed overnight had joined them as guides. Frazer knew the rainforest but he did not know the location of the fossil site.

They all put on their hats, tucked their trousers into their boots, and swung their packs onto their backs. Then they stepped into rainforest, following a tiny track, unnoticeable to anyone who didn't know it was there.

It wasn't long before someone was in trouble.

CHAPTER FOUR

Andrew Smart was kneeling on the path with his head in his hands. His shirt was stuck to his back with sweat.

'What is it, Andrew?' Matt's dad asked as they all caught up with him.

Andrew just shook his head.

'Have you been drinking enough water?' asked Frazer. 'I think you're probably dehydrated. You've lost a lot of fluid in perspiration already and we've only been going an hour and a half.'

Andrew took the water bottle Frazer handed him and drank well. Eventually, he nodded and got to his feet.

Matt's dad patted him on the back. 'None of us are used to this environment. Well, apart from Frazer and the locals.' He grinned.

Matt took the hint and unstrapped his own water bottle. He'd never drank so much water before – and it had never tasted so good! He could see that the guides were impatient to move on, but it was hard going. He glanced at Jo. She hadn't said much since they started, and was obviously saving her energy. She seemed to be looking at everything too, whether in awe or fear, Matt wasn't sure.

Jean, on the other hand, seemed to make a fuss about everything. She moaned and groaned at every insect or dangling branch, swiping at them crossly. Matt smiled, and silently thanked Jo for not being as annoying as Jean.

In many places the path was overgrown and Matt supposed the vegetation grew very quickly here. One of the guides had a machete which he used to hack at the tough undergrowth.

Matt and Jo trudged near the back of the group and, once or twice, Matt thought he heard something behind them. The rainforest was a noisy place, but this was not bird calls or monkeys chattering, it was more like the cracking of twigs as they were stepped on, and sometimes a low hum that could have been voices. He had a feeling that they were being watched, but the talk with Dad last night might have fuelled his imagination.

'What is it?' whispered Jo.

He shrugged. 'I just thought I heard something behind us, but I was probably wrong. The birds make such a racket.'

The word jaguar crossed his mind, but would it be stalking them? Frazer said animals generally got out of the way.

Andrew seemed better after his drink, and Matt noticed that he heeded Frazer's advice and kept having a swig. He was also talking to Jean quite a lot, as well as to Dad. Matt knew that both Jean and Andrew had been chosen by the Palaeontology Institute to come on this dig so they must each be well qualified and have their own special contribution to make to the expedition. Jean, though, still seemed to resent his and Jo's presence. She made no attempt at subtlety and wagged her finger at them whilst obviously complaining to both Andrew and Matt's dad. Maybe she considered that it somehow lessened the honour of being chosen by the Institute.

At last they stopped for some food, which the hotel had prepared for their first day. The guides cleared a small area so the party could take off their packs and sit down to rest their legs for a while.

Jo was looking worried and kept glancing about. Finally, she whispered something to Matt's dad, who spoke to Frazer.

'Ah yes,' said Frazer. 'If you need the toilet, don't go far off the track and try to find a clearing. Don't just step into the forest! We're all in this together so no need to be embarrassed. Always let someone know.'

Both Jo and Jean disappeared in different directions.

Jo was soon back, and flopped down wearily, making the most of the break, but soon the guides got up and prepared to leave.

'Jean's not back,' said Matt. He'd noticed that she'd been gone a long time but hadn't wanted to say anything. 'She went towards the river.'

He saw his dad frown, and Frazer spoke to the guides. Then they all went off together in the direction of the river, whose grey sluggish waters Matt had spotted from time to time through a rare break in the dense trees.

When Matt and Jo arrived at the river's edge, Jean was perched on a rock putting her socks and boots back on, and looking sheepish but indignant. Frazer berated her stupidity.

'The river was clear and very shallow,' Jean said firmly, tugging at her boot laces. 'I really had to cool off my feet and I could see that there was nothing in the water.'

'Piranhas can move faster than you,' said Frazer.

'There are also electric eels in these waters, as well as leeches and the occasional crocodile. I'm here to give you the benefit of my experience ...' He shook his head. 'If something happens to you it will affect the whole expedition. We are not exactly near civilisation.'

She had the sense to say nothing, and Matt noticed that she reddened and gritted her teeth when he caught her eye. Being told off in front of children was embarrassing, especially after having complained that they were here at all.

Matt couldn't help feeling smug. One point to them!

Just as they were turning from the river to return to the path, Jo said, 'What are all those logs floating down the river?'

They all turned and looked.

A huge stack of logs, bound together, was floating downstream, and behind it were several more, all tied together in a long chain.

'Illegal logging,' said Frazer. 'There's a lot of money in timber. The world's demand for wood for things like fuel and paper has only increased in recent years.'

The two guides seemed agitated and were trying to get them away and back to the path.

'They don't seem to want us to see,' said Matt's dad. 'Do you think they're in on it?'

'Could be. Either that, or they have been threatened into silence. It happens a lot. Most people in this area are poor. The loggers are paid well, and sometimes they have no choice. There isn't the easy access to healthcare or an education here or a steady income that we're used to, it is easy to see trees as just another natural resource to be exploited, like oil and gas elsewhere – a means of getting out of poverty.'

'What happens to the logs?' asked Matt.

'They float downstream to a town where there is road access. They often get sawn up into planks at a hidden mill somewhere, and then acquire forged papers to make them legal.'

Matt suddenly remembered the big tyre marks near their hotel in the town where they'd spent the night. Maybe that was where the logs were brought ashore and loaded onto trucks.

'That's terrible!' Jo surprised him by almost spitting the words. 'How can they do that? The world depends on the existence of this rainforest!' She looked from one to the other, as if waiting for an answer.

It was Andrew who gave it. 'Money,' he said. 'And greed. What do the people at the top care about the future?'

'It's their world, too,' said Jo. 'Don't they know that forests absorb carbon dioxide and give off oxygen? This is the last huge rainforest in the world. It's like the world's lungs ...'

'OK,' said Jean. 'We don't need a lesson in geography.'

'You have a satellite phone, Uncle Alan. Aren't you going to report them?' Jo persisted.

'That phone is for emergencies, Jo. I'll report it when we get back, but I guess the authorities know.'

Frazer nodded. 'They do, but they're only just beginning to realise what a big problem it is. The Amazon rainforest is a vast area to police.'

Jo just shook her head and glared back at the river. 'You don't seem to care much, Matt.'

'Of course I care. What can we do, though?' Matt was surprised. She might not have done her homework on the fossils they were searching for, but she seemed knowledgeable about the rainforest and conservation.

She was silent for a long time, swiping at the vegetation with a stick until Frazer asked her to stop.

Later, Matt again heard a scuffle behind them and the feeling that they were being followed returned. It was the odd footstep that didn't seem to fit, a bird frightened from a tree some way behind. Maybe it was someone from the loggers' camp, making sure they didn't report the logs. There was no ordinary mobile phone service here, although any group of trekkers would have a satellite phone in case of emergencies.

He remembered his dad's colleague from university, who had vowed to find the dinosaur eggs for himself. Did he know where the site was, or was he following them?

Matt considered telling his dad, but it would look foolish if there wasn't anyone, and maybe Dad didn't want the others to find out. No. He could find out for himself. If there was no-one, fine, but if they were being followed, he would be the one to warn Dad.

'Jo, I'm going to hang back and see if we're being followed. I'll pretend I need the loo.'

He was pleased that she didn't try to dissuade him, but gave a secret smile as though the trek wasn't exciting enough for her and this added a little extra. She seemed to have calmed down from earlier.

'Catch up as soon as you can, son,' said Dad.

Matt picked his way warily into the forest a little way, careful where he stepped, and remembering Frazer's advice. There was a small clearing around a tree and he looked up its straight trunk to the canopy of dense green overhead. Then he gave all his attention to the path, not quite knowing what he expected to see, or even what he would do if he saw someone – or something. As the minutes ticked by, Matt became aware of how far ahead the group must be getting, and how alone he was. He could feel his heart thudding and a wave of almost panic swept over him. It had been a silly idea. If they were being followed, it was by someone, or something, up to no good. What was he going to do about it?

Finally, he could stand it no longer, and pushed back through the undergrowth to the path. He looked back the way they had come but there was no sign of anything or anyone. It must be his imagination.

But when he turned back to continue ahead and catch up with the group, a slight movement on the path made him look more closely. Just in front of him, coiled right across the track, was a brownish green mottled snake. A lancehead.

CHAPTER FIVE

Matt's heart thumped and his mouth felt dry. He wished more than ever that he hadn't hung back. What a stupid idea that had been! Had he being trying to prove to the adults that he was a valued member of the team? Not like that stupid woman, Jean, who might be a great palaeontologist but was not a good team player.

The snake stirred and raised its head a little. Without taking his eyes off it, Matt took a step backwards, then another. When he felt he was out of striking distance, he yelled as loudly as he could.

There was no response. He realised that sound wouldn't travel too well in this dense forest, and that his yell would probably be indistinguishable from the bird cries.

The snake reared up a little more and Matt tried to gauge how far it could strike. Would his shouting frighten it? He didn't know. He imagined his dad coming back, with the rest of them. Now it would be him looking silly and holding up the expedition, reinforcing Jean's opinion.

Come on, Matt, he thought, you can't let a snake get the better of you. Frazer had said that creatures were frightened of humans. Their bite or sting was self-defence. This was their environment, after all.

He looked to see whether there was a way around the snake, but that meant walking into the dense undergrowth again. Better to face the one he could see.

Meanwhile, the others were getting further ahead. How long before he was really missed?

He had to shout again.

Stepping back slowly again, he yelled, 'Dad!' as loud as he could. He'd never shouted so loudly before.

The two guides were the first on the scene. The one with the machete indicated that Matt should move back further. Then, with one swift slash, he

45

cut the snake in two. The other man picked up the two halves and carried them away.

Matt took a deep breath and let it out slowly. His

head felt muzzy and his heart thumped.

'That was a scary moment, son.' His dad had hurried to the scene, looking pale and wiping his forehead with his sleeve. He put his hand on Matt's shoulder, obviously trying to play down the fright he'd got, but Matt could tell that he was angry, too.

'I thought you were more sensible than that, Matt. You know how important it is to follow the rules.'

'I thought we were being followed,' he whispered.

'You let me worry about that. Stop trying to be a hero and proving yourself. A useful expedition member looks out for his fellow members and stays alert for the good of all.'

'Sorry, Dad.' Matt knew he was guilty of doing exactly what he'd accused Jean of doing.

That evening, when they stopped for the night, the guides gutted, skinned and seasoned the snake, and then wrapped it in leaves and cooked it over the fire.

Matt thought that it tasted like chicken.

'You're one brave guy,' said Andrew, sitting down next to Matt, plate in hand. 'I've got a real phobia about snakes.'

'And yet you wanted to come and trek through the rainforest that is crawling with them?' Matt smiled up at the man. 'I'm more afraid of spiders.'

'Yeah, well, you've got to face your fears.'

'That's what being brave is,' said Jo. 'It's the same with bears in Canada. You have to back away slowly, and never look them in the eye.'

'Hard.' Andrew nodded.

'Yep.'

'Time to turn in. Early start tomorrow,' said Matt's dad.

'What's new?' muttered Matt.

Tomorrow they would arrive at the dig site, but for tonight it was tents in a clearing and swathes of mosquito netting. The guides poured a thin stream of salt around each tent, 'to protect them from snakes,' Frazer said.

'That's one worry less,' said Andrew, grinning to hide his fear, Matt thought. The only way to cope was to joke about it. Except for Frazer, he never joked.

Matt slept well. He wasn't used to doing so much walking, let alone in this heat. As he slowly woke up he was aware of the sunshine dappling through gaps in the canopy overhead and the thin walls of the tent, and he could hear the murmur of voices outside.

Then there was another sensation. It was a series of light pressures on his chest, as if ...

He opened his eyes slowly.

A large shape loomed in front of him. Something was standing on his chest. Something with many legs, and which spanned his own body.

As Matt's eyes sprang open his breath caught and he felt his heart race. A very large tarantula had somehow got under his mosquito net and was standing on his chest. It bounced very slightly and then lifted one front leg and waved it about, as if trying to decide whether or not to step forward. A couple more steps and it would be on Matt's face.

Matt was frozen, hardly daring to breath and hoping that his racing heart wouldn't disturb the spider. Frazer hadn't mentioned these – he was probably saving them for wee briefing number two. So Matt didn't know whether they were poisonous or not. He supposed the same rule applied as to the snake. Keep still. No sudden movements. Don't frighten it.

Was Dad still here on the bed next to him or had he got up already? Matt was afraid to move, even

turn his head. What should he do? He daren't call out. If he blew on the spider would it run, or bite? Maybe if he turned slowly onto his side it would run off. But then, spiders could climb sheer walls.

His mouth was dry and he felt light-headed. If he passed out there was no telling what he would do. He couldn't take much more of this. His eyes fixed on the spider's huge fangs.

Please go away. Please. I won't hurt you.

Matt was beginning to tremble and he knew the tarantula could feel it. It was becoming a bit restless and trying to rear up on its hind legs.

Just then, Matt heard his dad. The tent flap opened with a swish, which the spider registered with a small jump.

'Hey Matt! Wake up!' Then there was silence as his dad took in the situation.

'Don't move! I'll fetch someone.'

In a moment one of the local guides came in, holding a long stick. Before he could use it, however, the tarantula suddenly ran off Matt's chest, on to the floor, and out though the tent opening.

Matt had to hold back the tears of fright. Jo had appeared, and he wasn't going to let her see him cry.

His dad put his arm around him. 'Well done,

son,' he said. 'You were very brave to lie without moving.'

Frazer had joined them, too. 'Scary creatures,' he said. 'They can bite, but it's not life-threatening. What's worse is that they can flick hairs at you from their abdomen, and if they get in your eye it can be serious.' He looked puzzled. 'I can't imagine how it got under your net, though. Make sure that you tuck it securely under your sleeping mat.'

Matt knew that he had.

He was quiet throughout breakfast and only ate because his dad said he had to. In truth, he felt sick, but he knew that the rest of the trek would be pretty tough on an empty stomach. He was glad he hadn't known about the flicking hairs. Would he have kept his eyes shut? He doubted it.

The snake yesterday and the spider today. What next? he thought. He was grateful to Jo for not going on about it. He could feel her gaze on him from time to time, but she said nothing.

He wondered for the second time whether his dad was regretting letting him and Jo come, especially now that they had competition. Dad certainly had a worried look on his face most of the time. Was his fellow student following them, or had he hired guides, as they had? They must be getting near the dig site now.

The morning trek was uneventful and Matt began to relax. They had a short break at noon, and soon afterwards the guides stopped and turned to Frazer. The three had a brief discussion and Matt watched as they pointed towards the river and Frazer nodded.

Matt looked at his dad. His brow was lined with tiredness. In fact, everyone looked as though they had had enough. None of them were used to sustained walking, especially under these conditions.

'Right.' It was Frazer. 'The dig site is near here on the other side of the river.' He indicated that they should follow as the guides cut through the undergrowth towards the faint sound of water.

'Do we have to cross the river?' Jo looked alarmed.

'It looks like it,' said Matt.

'We'll see,' said his dad. 'Our guides are locals so they will know what to do.'

Matt looked at Jo. He couldn't blame her for being apprehensive.

CHAPTER SIX

The river was brown and sluggish and about ten metres wide with thick undergrowth growing right to the edge on this side, although Matt could see a wide beach area on the opposite bank, and behind that some rough-hewn steps leading up to a higher cleared area on which stood several cabins.

He was aware of a slight droning noise, but didn't pay much attention. Tied up to a tree on their side was a simple wooden raft. No wading through then, he thought with relief.

'Our guides will go across with the raft rope and secure it on the other side. Then we can pull ourselves across,' said Frazer. 'Don't worry. They've done this before. They will choose a spot where the water is still, and then wade

across, disturbing it as little as possible. Actually, piranhas rarely attack humans, but crocodiles do, and also electric eels.'

'And the wish-you-were-dead fish,' said Jo.

Frazer gave one of his rare smiles and nodded.

Matt shuddered, glad that they didn't have to do it. The river didn't look all that shallow, and the fact that piranhas rarely attacked humans wasn't enough for him.

They all watched in silence as the two local men studied the river carefully. Then they stepped into the water, watching every step of the way. Once they paused, staring hard at something in the water. Then they slowly waded further in, the water getting higher and higher up their legs until they were more than waist-deep.

This was the critical time, when they couldn't move quickly. Their faces were expressionless, but Matt could see that they were focussed. He imagined how difficult it must be to wade slowly.

Then they were past the middle and soon

climbing out onto the little beach, where they secured the raft rope to a tree.

Each person seemed to let out a breath of relief as the guides turned and gave a wave.

Gingerly, one by one, the other six climbed onto the raft. Jean and Jo both stumbled as Frazer and Matt's dad tried to hold the thing steady.

'It would be best to sit down, I think,' said Matt.

When they were all aboard, Andrew began pulling the rope, hauling them little by little across the river. Although the current looked sluggish, as they reached the middle of the river

it was obvious that he was struggling to hold it from being dragged downstream.

Something moved or shimmered. Was it a trick of the light? Matt held his breath, remembering what this river held. Crocodiles, slow and sly until they needed speed. One snap of those jaws and the raft would be matchsticks.

'Let me help,' said Matt's dad, crawling forward and grabbing hold of the rope, too.

The dark shape stayed still, and it was only when they passed over it that Matt saw that it was just a rock. He hadn't realised that he was still holding his breath, and let it out with a whoosh.

He wasn't the only one who was relieved when they finally reached the shore and clambered out. Jo looked strained and silent, too. His dad and Andrew dragged the raft well up on the beach.

'No, no!' Frazer held up his hand. 'These guys have to return it to the other side for anyone using the path. We'll be leaving by helicopter, remember.'

'Is the helicopter going to land here, Dad?' Matt pointed to the beach they were standing on.

'Yes, that's the idea. It's not easy but flat enough. But we have some work to do first. You'll be pleased to know that we have cabins to sleep in while we're here. They're used by the travel companies who organise rainforest treks. Remember, it was people on one of those treks who first discovered the amazonsaurus fossils.'

'Check your cabins for inhabitants,' said Frazer over his shoulder as they followed him up the rough steps that Matt had spotted from the other side of the river.

'And he doesn't mean holiday-makers,' said Jo with a grimace. She stopped. 'What's that?'

As they had reached the plateau, the faint noise that Matt had heard became louder. It sounded like a giant prehistoric dragonfly.

'I think it's a chainsaw,' he muttered.

The loggers weren't far away.

He watched Jo's face as it registered with her.

'They're right near us! I can't believe ...'

'Jo, you and Jean can have this cabin.' Matt was glad that Dad had interrupted Jo, but she was right. How could they stop the loggers? But anyway, he had bigger things to worry about. He still wasn't sure if they were being followed.

It was obvious that Jean was not pleased with the idea of sharing with Jo any more than Jo was. They both stomped off towards their cabin and Matt smiled as he watched

Jean gingerly open the door and then hesitate, before Jo stepped forward, bravely. She was going up in Matt's estimation by the minute!

And yes! Things were getting better all round. Tomorrow was the start of their real reason for being here: to find some amazonsaurus eggs. Dad had to find the eggs, and not just because Frank Hellman was on his tail: he'd promised the Brazilian government a painting of the creature in return for their funding. That was where Matt's gift came in. He had to hold an egg to see what this dinosaur was really like. Thinking about it reminded him that Jo didn't know his secret, and he wasn't even sure that he wanted her to know yet. She probably wouldn't believe him. The only people who knew about it were Mum and Dad, but now that he would be accompanying his father on expeditions, he wouldn't be able to keep it a secret for much longer. He wondered how people might react. He imagined trying to sit through a maths class at school with photographers and journalists pressed up against the windows. Maths might be boring, but he didn't fancy sharing every moment of his life with newspapers either!

The site of the dig was just a little way from the river, on a flat open area of soft sandstone. It was obvious where the fossils had been removed, and

Jean and the men put down their bag of tools and surveyed the area.

'How will they know where to look for eggs?' asked Jo.

'They won't. There may not even be any. We don't know if the dinosaur found was a male or female or if there are any nests nearby.'

'They must be really big, the eggs, I mean.'

'The biggest are about the size of a football,' said Matt. 'Even though the adults were enormous there is a limit to how big the eggs can be because the bigger they are, the thicker the shell would have to be, and then the baby wouldn't be able to crack it.'

Jo nodded, scraping at the ground with her shoe. He could tell that something was bothering her.

'Let's go and help,' he said. 'The eggs can be round or oval and will look like big stones. We've only got a few days here so we have a better chance of finding one if we all look. Anyway, what else are we going to do, have a swim in the river?'

'I wish we could,' she said.

They both heard the whine of the chainsaws starting up.

Jo's mouth set in a determined look. 'Before we

leave,' she said,' I've got to do something about that!'

Matt laughed aloud. He'd known she was going to be a pain. 'You! What do you think you can do? Well, I'm going to do what we're here for. Dad didn't pay for you to come with us just to go off on some campaign of your own.'

As soon as he'd spoken, he regretted how it had sounded. Of course he agreed with her, but they were just a couple of kids. What could they do?

'I said, before we leave. Right now I'm egg hunting. So, what did this dinosaur look like?'

Matt just looked at her. He'd known she hadn't bothered to do any research before they came. That's how interested she was.

'It's called Amazonsaurus maranhensis.' Matt's dad approached them. 'The last bit refers to this province. It was a sauropod. They had very long necks, long tails, small heads, and thick, pillar-like legs, and were herbivores. They were about twelve metres long and weighed up to four tons. Not the biggest ones of their kind by far, but unusual to be found here in this climate, although in their day it was hot and dry here and South America was still joined onto Africa.'

Matt scowled as his Dad handed Jo a series of small tools she could use to help. He took his

own rucksack from his back and removed the items he decided he would need: a small trowel and a soft brush.

They began to dig and sift through the sandy soil carefully, examining any stones or rocks, brushing each gently so as not to damage what may be an ancient fossil. Matt showed Jo how to do it, and then kept an eye on anything she found. She'd had no experience of digging for fossils and he couldn't blame her for not recognising one.

There was no sign of the rival team and Dad hadn't mentioned them at all. Maybe they hadn't been serious. Nevertheless, the raft was now back on the other side of the river just waiting to be used. Shouldn't Dad have suggested it stay on this side? Maybe that would have led to too many explanations.

They worked on, thankful for some shade from the trees, remembering to take frequent drinks of water.

They didn't find anything that day or the next, but that was generally the way of fossil hunting. You needed patience and luck, just as much as instinct and knowledge. It was Thursday and the helicopter was booked to pick them up on Saturday. The funding was limited, as well as Matt's dad being committed to other work. He was so much in demand and it would be a shame if they'd come this far for nothing.

The buzz of the chainsaws seemed to be getting nearer and Matt noticed that Jo became more restless. She kept breaking off from her work and frowning, looking towards where the sound was coming from. Her expression was a mixture of anger and sadness. Once or twice she mumbled something that Matt couldn't hear, but he guessed the gist.

On Friday morning she said, 'I've got to go and stop them. Somehow.'

'But you don't speak Portuguese,' reasoned Matt. 'And even if you did, do you think they would listen to you? You're not the only one who will have tried to do something. Where there's big money there's danger to anyone who gets in their way.'

Jo waved her hand in dismissal. 'You watch too much TV. I can't just do nothing, even if you can.'

'These men aren't the ones to blame, it's those higher up who sell the timber.'

Matt thought about telling his dad, but Jo had picked up her trowel again and knelt down to scrape at the soil. Maybe she was just getting fed up. You had to be certain kind of person to do this job. She'd made her point. She was opposed to illegal logging and the clearing of the rainforest. Who wasn't? He remembered the prehistoric scene when he'd held the titanosaurus egg. Habitat was being destroyed then, not by man, but by the earth itself, the movement of the tectonic plates causing volcanic eruptions.

That was evolution. This was madness and greed. Secretly, he totally agreed with Jo.

And in the early afternoon, she disappeared.

CHAPTER SEVEN

She couldn't have been gone long, Matt guessed. Maybe he could bring her back without anyone knowing she'd ever been gone. But he knew as he sneaked away from the dig that it was a mistake. Firstly, they'd been told not to go into the rainforest alone, and secondly, why was he trying to prevent her from getting into trouble? He risked not only danger, but his dad's anger and that of the whole team, but perhaps he could stop Jo before she caused even more trouble for them. Who knew what the loggers were capable of if someone interfered?

Matt followed the sound of the chainsaws, making his way carefully through the scrub. It wasn't so much forest here as thick vegetation. Maybe this area had been cleared of trees already.

He watched each step in front of him, pushing the leaves back with a long stick, careful where he put his feet. The memory of that lancehead was still fresh in his mind.

There was no sign of Jo, but she couldn't have been gone that long. She hadn't managed to stop the tree felling yet, either, he thought smugly. Those chainsaws were getting louder.

When he reached the site, it took him by surprise. Suddenly, a huge space opened up in front of him. It was a large bald patch in the forest, bereft of anything, even a blade of grass; shaved clean except for the stumps of the felled trees.

Great piles of logs waited by the river to be sent on their way. Enormous machines gathered up the fallen logs and transported them to make new piles. At the far end of the clearing the felling was taking place. Now Matt could hear the actual noise of the trees falling. With one creak and crash, something that had taken hundreds of years to grow, was gone forever.

Then a machine stripped off the branches and chopped the trunks into lengths.

It was a sorry sight. Like some sort of battle, with an army cutting down its enemy – one that couldn't fight back or even run. This vast army of trees was at the mercy of the men who were driven by both poverty and greed.

Then Matt saw Jo. She was standing dangerously near to where the felling was happening, and she was shouting. As Matt watched, one of the men stopped his chainsaw and waved it at her, shouting back, indicating that she should get out of the way. She stood her ground, and Matt had to admire her for that. Although it was very foolish, he felt proud of her too.

A group of men started towards her and she ran and climbed up one of the log piles at the edge of the river.

'Jo!' Matt yelled. 'It's useless.' But he ran towards

her, clambering up the log pile after her, and feeling it shift a little. 'You've made your point, Jo. You've done your best,' he panted, reaching the top of the pile to stand beside h e r .

'This was a brave thing to do.'

Jo glared at him and opened her mouth to speak but just then there was another movement beneath them that made them almost lose their balance. Then another jolt, and a bigger movement. They both fell down on their knees.

'We've got to get off here, Jo! The logs are moving.'

Jo seemed to see the danger they were in, and nodded. But it was too late. As they began to clamber down the side of the pile Matt's foot slipped. His heart skipped a beat and he clung on desperately until he found a foothold again, but by now the log pile, bound together by thick rope, was already floating out into the middle of the river and being caught by the current.

CHAPTER EIGHT

As Matt looked back at the logging site, he saw that the men had stopped working and were watching with frightened faces as he and Jo clung to the log pile. There was nothing they could do, nothing anyone could do. They were at the mercy of the river and had no means of steering or controlling the log raft at all.

'Matt.' Jo looked at him with terrified eyes, all the fire gone out of her. 'What are we going to do?'

Matt just stared back at her, feeling numb with fear. In front to them lay miles of river before they reached the town where they'd stayed overnight, and who knew what the river was like along the way? Although they'd been following it they had only had glimpses of it. There could be rapids or waterfalls, for all he knew. And even when they

reached the town it might be the middle of the night and no-one would see or hear them.

He shuddered. Then a thought came to him.

'Jo! We'll pass the dig site! Get ready to yell your head off.'

'And what can they do?'

'At least they'll know where we are. They might think of something.' Matt knew it was a small chance. They had to try.

The log pile buffeted against rocks, but didn't slow. Instead it jolted the pair backwards and forwards, until they clung onto each other as well as the pile.

'We're nearly there! Look. That's where we crossed the river. There's that little beach.'

They got ready to yell and wave with one hand if they could. The dig site was coming up now.

But it was deserted.

'Where are they? Where is everyone?' Jo whispered, barely audible above the sound of the rushing river beneath them.

Matt could feel tears prick his eyes. He spun on Jo. 'They're probably out looking for us! I knew you should never have come!'

Jo hung her head, but he couldn't see whether

she was crying or not. Again, he regretted being so sharp.

The raft had picked up speed. For a moment he thought they might be able to jump, but the idea of piranhas, electric eels and crocodiles soon put that thought out of his mind. He wasn't brave enough for that.

Jo stood up suddenly. 'Matt!' She was pointing. Ahead the branch of a tree leaned out over the river. 'Do you think we can grab that?'

'If we miss we'll be knocked into the water.'

'We have to try, Matt.' Her eyes were alive again, hopeful.

They had to make a decision quickly. If she was brave enough …

'Let's do it!' Matt said.

They stood next to each other waiting to reach the branch. Were they travelling too fast? Would they just be knocked off the log raft like a crumb off a table?

They stood with their arms outstretched waiting to reach the tree, trying to judge its height, hoping the current wouldn't sweep them in another direction at the last minute. It was a thick bough, rough and covered with creeper and moss. What if it was rotten? What if it disintegrated at their touch?

Matt didn't have time to think about that. 'Ready!' He took a deep breath. 'Now!'

The branch slammed into his chest, almost knocking the wind out of his lungs. It was certainly not rotten. He felt the wet moss and his fingers tangled in the creeper. For a moment he grappled to find a hold. Then he was swinging in the air and the log raft was sailing on without them.

'Jo.' He turned. She was there, swinging her way to shore. Matt felt such a relief that he almost relaxed too much and lost his grip. She even gave a little giggle.

They stood on the bank shaking, almost crying, but not quite.

'You can't beat the loggers!' said Matt, quietly. 'You can yell at them all you like but it won't make any difference. You may well have just sabotaged this whole expedition for your crusade!'

Jo opened her mouth to reply but must have thought better of it. She gave a slight nod and they set off following the river bank, stepping through almost impenetrable vegetation, mindful of snakes, until they reached the dig site.

It was still deserted, but they could hear voices. So the others were not out looking for them after all.

Just beyond the dig site, just out of sight of the river, the team stood in a group. In front of them about ten men had them corralled against the cliff face. They didn't seem to be armed, but they certainly looked threatening.

'Matt! Jo! You're safe!' Matt's dad took a step forward, but was barred from coming any nearer by a couple of the men.

'Who ...' Matt began, but he knew who they were, and he could see why. On the ground lay three dinosaur eggs.

'So you're his son,' said the man who was obviously in charge, turning to look at Matt. 'But your trip has been in vain. We shall be taking these eggs that you have kindly located for us. But your father is being a bit uncooperative. Still, there are more of us ...' He motioned to three of his men to pick up the eggs and then smirked at Matt. 'I hope you enjoyed your visitor last night. Not enough to put you off? Maybe your father will realise that this is no place for children.'

'You're still a failure, Frank Hellman,' said Matt's dad. 'This is not what palaeontology is all about. It's about furthering our knowledge and sharing our findings with the world. Your motives are revenge and self-glorification. And frightening young boys is plain cowardly.'

'It's my turn now, Sharp.' He prodded a finger into Matt's dad's chest, then turned and gave an order. 'Launch the boats.'

Matt watched as several men dragged two small boats out of the undergrowth and towards the river.

It looked as though he was never going to get to hold one of the eggs.